T0207867

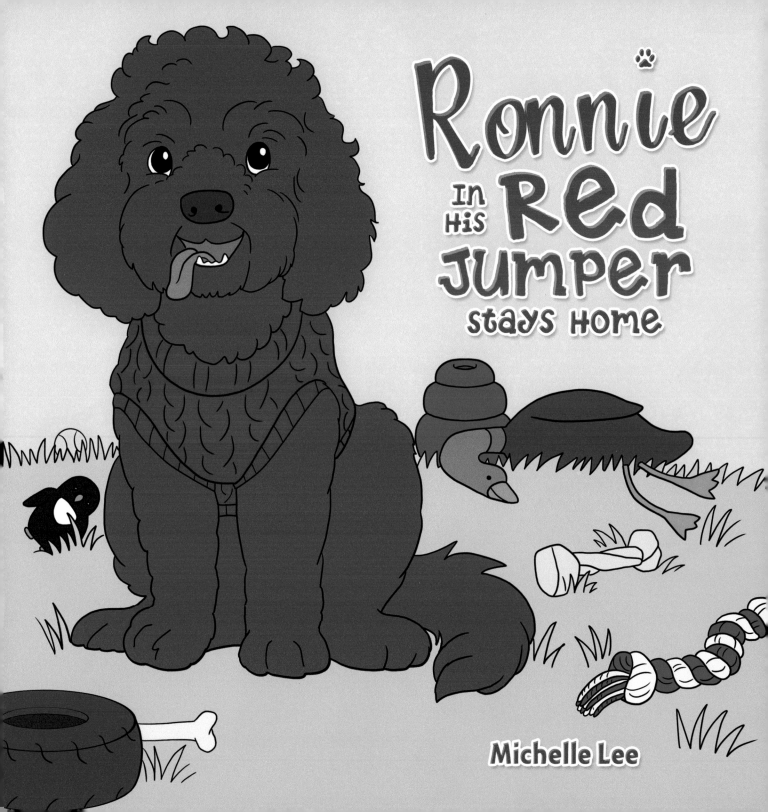

Ronnie In His Red Jumper Stays Home

Michelle Lee

AuthorHouse™ UK
1663 Liberty Drive
Bloomington, IN 47403 USA
www.authorhouse.co.uk
UK TFN: 0800 0148641 (Toll Free inside the UK)
UK Local: 02036 956322 (+44 20 3695 6322 from outside the UK)

Because of the dynamic nature of the Internet, any web addresses or links contained in this book may have changed
since publication and may no longer be valid. The views expressed in this work are solely those of the author and do not
necessarily reflect the views of the publisher, and the publisher hereby disclaims any responsibility for them.

Any people depicted in stock imagery provided by Getty Images are models,
and such images are being used for illustrative purposes only.
Certain stock imagery © Getty Images.

This book is printed on acid-free paper.

ISBN: 978-1-6655-9334-2 (sc)
ISBN: 978-1-6655-9333-5 (e)

Print information available on the last page.

Published by AuthorHouse 09/15/2021

authorHOUSE®

Ronnie
In His Red Jumper
stays Home

Marnie and Ronnie love to go out,
walking on their leads or
running freely about.

But today they're at home thinking,
"What can we do?"

"I have an idea," barked Ronnie,
"Let's hide Millie's shoe?"

Marnie let out an almighty yawn,

"I was doing all that before
you were born."

"A nap," Ronnie barked,
"You go ahead,

I'll play by myself in the
house instead."

Marnie curled up and
thought, "It will be ok,
letting Ronnie play alone
in the house all day."

With Marnie asleep Ronnie
began to explore.

He crept upstairs and
nudged open the door.

He went into the bathroom,
he had so much fun!

"Uh oh Ronnie, what have you done?"

He went into Millie's bedroom,
he had so much fun!

"Uh oh Ronnie, what have you done?"

Suddenly, Ronnie heard
keys at the door.

He crawled out from under
the mess on the floor.

Millie gave him a cuddle and asked, "Have you had fun?"

The End

Printed in the United States
by Baker & Taylor Publisher Services